The BOY WHO ATE STARS

This book is supported by the French Ministry for Foreign Affairs, as part of the Burgess programme, headed for the French Embassy in London by the Institute Français du Royaume-Uni.

Liberté • Égalité • Fraternité
RÉPUBLIQUE FRANÇAISE

THE BOY WHO ATE STARS

K O C H K A

Translated by Sarah Adams

EGMONT

A Matthieu, mon ange.

First published in Great Britain 2004
by Egmont Books Ltd
239 Kensington High Street, London W8 6SA
First published in France 2002
By Éditions Grasset & Fasquelle, Paris
French title: *L'enfant qui caressait les cheveux*

Copyright in the original text © 2002 Éditions Grasset & Fasquelle
Copyright in the English translation © 2004 Sarah Adams
Cover photograph copyright © 2004 Robert Dawson/Getty Images

The moral rights of the author and translator have been asserted

ISBN 1 4052 1129 6

3 5 7 9 10 8 6 4 2

A CIP catalogue record for this title is available from the British Library

Typeset by Avon DataSet Ltd, Bidford on Avon, Warwickshire
Printed and bound in Great Britain by the CPI Group

I'm Lucy and I live in Paris. When I grow up, I want to teach autistic children. I know one already, he's called Matthew and he's my neighbour. Matthew was four when he came into my life and, to be honest, we got off to a rocky start. Now I see a lot of him, and each time I can't help thinking how special he is because he's like nobody I've ever met.

CHAPTER 1

It all began with us moving to 11 Rue Merlin.
Our flat's on the fourth floor, left hand side. It
was September, I was twelve and I didn't know
anybody. But I'd promised myself something: I was
going to get to know all my neighbours. I'd even
got a plan of action. Once school started again, I'd
work my way from the ground floor to the top,
and pin up flags in my bedroom for the different
countries everyone came from. There were lots of
foreign-sounding names on the letterboxes, so I

was hoping for a big catch. My theme for the year was going to be global encounters. Until I met Matthew, that is. When he popped up in my life, he turned all my plans upside down and inside out.

It was the first Saturday evening since the start of Year 8. Our neighbours in the upstairs flat were making a lot of noise, so Dad put on his dressing gown like someone loading a gun and headed up to see what was going on. He was so annoyed he didn't bother with the lift, but charged up the stairs instead. So, even though I was curious to find out what was going on too, I waited on the doormat.

Marie opened the door. I'd seen her before in the downstairs lobby and I recognised her gentle voice. Marie is Matthew's mother. I was listening out for a neighbour's spat I could tell everyone about at school . . . but I didn't hear a thing. No raised voices. No cross words either. Dad came back down a few minutes later looking like everything was fine and sorted. He and Mum spoke in hushed whispers, and then he switched topics. But what beat me was there was still lots of banging coming from upstairs. So the next day, on my way out to buy our baguette for breakfast, I decided to go up.

There was a funny drawing of a child, with hands as huge as wings and big ears too, pinned to the front door of the fifth floor flat. I didn't have a clue what I was going to say, but I rang anyway. A woman I'd never seen before opened the door. She was old enough to be Marie's mother, but she didn't look like her. I said, 'Hello.' (Mum claims I'm never one to hold back.) The woman smiled and stepped aside to let me through. She gave me a warm welcome but didn't say anything, which felt weird for someone chatty like me. The front door opened on to a corridor with a long Oriental rug. I was about to introduce myself when Matthew appeared.

'He was handsome, he was blond, he smelled of delicious warm sand ...' The moment I saw him at the bottom of the corridor, those lyrics came into my head. Actually, Matthew's got brown

curly hair, he's short and pale and he doesn't look anything like 'My Legionnaire' in the Serge Gainsbourg song Mum's always singing. But he's so handsome there *should* be a song about him.

Matthew bolted out of nowhere like a mad dog and jumped on top of me, nearly knocking me over, before ending up on tiptoes with both hands in my hair. He skilfully ran his fingers all over my head, squealing and making occasional *'fshhttt!'* noises. Matthew was on cloud nine, sending my hair flying in every direction and choking with laughter. He got so worked up he started chanting, 'You're playing with hair. You're playing with hair . . .' That's when the woman stepped in.

Still smiling and without saying a word, she pulled Matthew towards her, offering him her head instead, and Matthew changed heads. I mean, he let go of my hair and plunged his hands into the woman's. He took off her hair band and rumpled her loose hair. She's got straight blonde hair, but he didn't seem to notice the difference. Matthew dived right in with his hands and his fingers rose to the surface. He laughed and ran off.

Then came the calm after the storm. The woman picked up her hair band, smoothed her hair and tied it back up. Even the Oriental rug became royal again. I was the only one who was lost, and when the woman looked at me to find out what I wanted I was dumbstruck, which was a first for me. In the end, I stammered something about coming back later and rushed off. The way the woman closed the door peacefully behind me, you'd think nothing had happened. So it was almost a relief to see my messed-up hair in the lift mirror.

Back out on the pavement, my legs ran in the direction of the bakery but my head was still up on the fifth floor. I bought the baguette. As luck would have it, Marie was also hurrying home. She saw me and held the door. I ran over and said 'Hello!' and then 'Mrs . . .?' in the hope we'd carry on talking.

She held out her hand, 'Hello there,' she introduced herself. 'I'm Marie. And you must be my new neighbour in the flat below.'

I nodded and gave her a big smile. Even though there was a big age gap, she was treating me as an equal. She seemed very kind. 'My name's Lucy,' I said after a pause. 'Don't worry about the noise last night, by the way. I managed to get to sleep in the end.'

When I realised how I must have sounded, I wished I could swallow my words back. Why do I always open my mouth too soon? I was worried she'd think I was trying to criticise her, which wasn't what I'd meant at all. But luckily, Marie understood perfectly. 'Pleased to meet you, Lucy,' she said, when the lift got to my floor. 'Sometimes Matthew gets a bit out of hand. Matthew's my son. He's autistic, but we're making progress. It just takes time.'

I could tell from her answer how warm and loving and full of hope she was. But that's all I got, because I didn't know the meaning of the key word in her sentence.

Mum thought I'd taken my time buying the baguette.

chapter 2

Sunday's the only day of the week when we eat breakfast together as a family. As usual, I put my foot in it.

'What does autistic mean?' I asked point-blank.

By the time you're twelve, it's important to have your own take on things. From a trip to the doctor's, I remembered that 'otitis' means ear infection, so I was expecting 'autistic' to have something to do with ears.

'You've been eavesdropping again!' Dad

accused me, once he'd got over his initial
surprise. Parents can't cope with you asking them
too many questions. They don't want you
growing up too quickly. I was in for a scene.

Mum: 'You can't *not* answer, or all sorts of
doubts creep in.'

Dad: 'But how's she going to understand?'

Mum: 'It doesn't matter, keep it simple, but
give her an answer!'

So Dad turned to me and said, 'An autistic
person is somebody who's different.' And his
head disappeared into his cup of coffee.

'Really?' I played stupid. 'Different? So you
mean they've got big ears?'

On second thoughts, maybe this was too
heavy a topic for a Sunday morning. Whatever,
Dad got annoyed, went to find the dictionary,
flicked through it in a temper and said flatly,

Autistic: suffering from autism.

He paused, and I thought he was going to stop
right there, which would have taken the biscuit.
But he carried on.

Autism (from the Greek, autos, oneself): a pathological withdrawal into an interior world resulting in a loss of contact with reality and an inability to communicate with others.

He read out this definition twice, to make a point of how patient he was being, before generously pointing out that, 'pathological means abnormal or unusual: an unusual withdrawal into an interior world resulting in a loss of contact etc . . .' Satisfied with his performance, he handed me the dictionary and went back into the kitchen.

Which left me sitting there wondering what such an obscure definition could mean. If you ask me, going to school teaches you that parents are the ones who need educating. So I decided to ask Marie. After all, she'd mentioned the difficult word in the first place. It was time to pay another visit to my neighbours upstairs.

I spotted my chance when Mr and Mrs De

Marotte de Montigny came round to tea with François. The De Marotte de Montignys (I just call them the Marottes, because you've got to draw the line somewhere), come round for tea every Sunday. I've never understood what my parents see in them. Mrs Marotte is a total airhead who's always blabbering. Mr Marotte never opens his mouth. Thank goodness there's François to save the day, even if he *is* as shy as a mouse. François is their dog, but they treat him like a fashion accessory. He's tiny, body-shy and trained to shuffle along without touching anything.

It was the first time the Marottes had visited us in our new flat. Mrs Marotte started tittering, Mr Marotte didn't say a word and François just stared at me. Poor animal. I felt sorry for him from the moment I saw him walking with his nose held high because he wasn't allowed to sniff things. That's no life for a dog. I tried making his owners see this, but I didn't get anywhere. Then I wondered about complaining to the RSPCA, because there are heavy fines for not respecting your pets' rights. It's like slavery. But on second thoughts, I decided to fight back. Secretly, I was going to take that dog under my wing so he could learn to fly.

I only had an hour a week to iron out his bad habits. My aim? To make him into a real dog during that hour. What mattered was getting François to discover his wild side. I wanted him to feel like a wolf. He needed to fill up his animal reserves so he could last the rest of the week.

I went slowly to start with, because I didn't want to scare him off. Realising you've got to start again from scratch is tough. And François was suspicious. I used to take him to the square where all the dogs meet up. But he would stay on his little patch, wiping his paws in embarrassment. Then, as time went by, he started wagging his tail and when he came to visit us there was a sparkle in his eye. I was very proud. Putting the zing back into somebody isn't easy.

So as I was saying, it was the first time the Marottes had come to our new flat and I suggested taking François out for a walk. Mrs Marotte agreed as long as we weren't too long, and they watched us set off. I tried to appear sensible and responsible, and François tiptoed along like a house dog.

But as soon as the door closed behind us, François jumped into my arms. He's a great dog. He wasn't muddled by our change of address.

We took the stairs. The drawing on the fifth floor door looked more intriguing than ever. I rang.

Marie opened the door.

'Sorry to bother you,' I began, 'but I've come about what you said . . . You know, about your autistic son . . . I looked it up in the dictionary, but the definition's a bit hard for someone my age. Could you explain it to me?'

Marie took her time, thinking about her answer in silence. It was quiet in the flat. Finally, she was ready. 'Matthew will be back soon,' she said. 'He's gone out with Maougo. Autism is a complicated subject you know.'

At first, I thought she was avoiding the issue,

but she carried on, 'I'd be very happy to talk to you about it, but not on the doormat. Why don't you come to supper one evening?'

'Do you really mean it?' I asked, not really believing her.

She suggested the following Friday. So she did mean it after all! 'No problem,' I replied. Bliss. I was going get to know the flat beyond the corridor with the Persian rug. That rug's like a river and it made me want to follow its flow. So, already preparing for our evening together, I asked, 'Is the woman I saw this morning with blonde hair your mother?'

'No,' Marie answered, 'but she almost could be.' And she went on: 'Maougo comes from Russia, and she doesn't speak French. I've only known her for two years, but she's changed my life.'

Marie explained how tired she used to get. Her maternity leave was coming to an end and since she was a single mother bringing up her little boy, she had to go back to work as a librarian. But no crèche would take her anti-social, hyperactive, noisy son. So Marie advertised and Maougo answered.

'To start with,' said Marie, 'she only came in the mornings, but it was such a relief to have her around that I asked her to move in with us. She's been our guardian angel ever since, she's like family.'

Just then, the lift stopped on their floor and Matthew jumped out. Maougo followed him calmly. But when Matthew saw François and me in front of his open door he stopped in his tracks, then he started shouting and doing some kind of dance. If I break it down, it went something like this . . .

1. He put his head in his hands
2. He stretched his arms up towards the ceiling
3. He threw himself to the floor
4. He spun round and round.

It was like a Native American dance to the cries of wolves. I was rooted to the spot. I had a sneaky feeling we were the cause of it all. All what? I didn't know. But it had to be something awful because he was calling on the sky and the earth. What really amazed me was that Matthew managed to fill the whole space, even though he's less than a metre tall.

Maougo was behind Matthew, bringing up the rear because she's safe as a fire door. She signalled to Marie who said, 'Bye, Lucy. See you on Friday!' and closed the door. I didn't have a clue what was going on. I'd clean forgotten about François in that whirlwind, and when I turned to look at him I was gobsmacked. That frightened little mouse, who dived under my legs every time he heard a strange noise, was standing firm and looking sympathetic.

> Sympathy (from the Greek, sumpatheia. From 'sun' meaning 'with' and 'pathein' meaning 'to feel'): An instinctive inclination that carries two people towards each other. Participation in joy and grief, a feeling of benevolence.

François' heart had gone out to Matthew. It was as if they understood each other. Was there some kind of code between them I didn't know about? As time went by, I saw that what brought Matthew so close to animals was being true to his own instincts.

I don't know how the scene ended, because we had to leave. Mum says events sometimes take a turn for the worse. Dad talks about things spinning out of control. We'd just seen something along those lines. But perhaps they acted out a different version after we left: Matthew and Maougo get out of the lift. The landing's clear. They ring. Marie opens the door. In they go.

Back on my own floor, the teapot was empty and the Marottes were waiting for François. 'My goodness, it's almost as if you haven't been outside at all!' Mrs Marotte gushed. But she still got the scented wipes out of her bag and started cleaning every inch of her dog that might have come into contact with the outside world. I laughed to myself because she looked so silly. Dealing with how an animal thinks is much more subtle than dealing with dirt, because thinking doesn't leave any marks. But I knew that one day François would be himself, it was just a question of time.

Once their pet was safely decontaminated, our friends took their leave. 'See you soon!' I called out. François barked. Yes! He was starting to learn how to express himself.

When I went to bed, I thought about my goals for the week ahead . . .

1. Find a way of telling my parents about the invitation for Friday.
2. Do some research about autism.

And with that, I fell asleep.

Over the next few days, I asked my class teacher about autism. She didn't want to give me her opinion, claiming she didn't know enough about the subject. I talked to Theodora, my first new friend. We spotted each other on the first day and we knew we'd get on.

'Austism?' said Theodora. 'No idea.' But when I told her about the battle of the hair, she tried running her hands through her own hair. And when I got to the bit about the shouting whirlwind, she started spinning.

'It's gentle,' she said, 'and it makes your head spin.'

I had a go, too. She was right. It was gentle and it made your head spin. It wasn't such a big deal. Out in the playground, we spun like tops and some of the other kids came over and started clapping us.

By Thursday, I still hadn't mentioned my plans for the following evening to my parents. I hadn't found the right moment. But time was running out. Luckily, Mum and I ran into Marie that evening.

'Hello,' she said, 'you must be Lucy's mother . . .'

Once they'd got their 'pleased to meet you's out of the way, Marie asked me straight out, 'Are you still OK for tomorrow, Lucy?'

When she saw me looking awkward and stuck for words, she turned to Mum. 'I've asked Lucy a favour. I was wondering if she'd agree to a regular slot – perhaps on a Friday evening since she doesn't have school on Saturdays – when she could spend some time with us. My son Matthew is autistic. He's four. But unlike most autistic children, he talks . . .'

With every word, Marie was trying to make Mum feel more at ease. I still didn't know what autism meant, but I realised we shouldn't make it sound too weird.

'. . . Apparently his intelligence is unaffected,' she went on. 'And he doesn't hurt himself, unlike some autistic children. I think I'd even go so far as to say he's happy . . . But the problem is he tends to be happy all by himself. We need to encourage him to become more sociable. That's where I thought Lucy might be able to help us out . . . That's if she'd like to, of course, and you don't have a problem with it. Sometimes children understand each other best, and Lucy is just right because she's between our age and Matthew's . . .'

Fantastic! Marie had got me out of a tight spot. She'd made it sound like I was the one doing them a favour, so there was no way Mum could say no.

It was my turn next, so I tried to sound level-headed. 'I'm definitely up for it. I've thought long and hard about it and it'd be my pleasure.'

So that's why I started spending a lot of time on the fifth floor of 11 Rue Merlin. It's also how Marie became my best grown-up friend.

CHAPTER 4

The next day dragged on. The only thing Theo and I talked about was the evening ahead. Minutes seemed to stretch into hours, but at last the long wait was over.

I decided to wear my hair down, but I changed my mind at the last minute and tied it up in a bun. That way, Matthew could have more fun making a mess of it. Mum was intrigued to see me taking so long getting ready. When it was time, I picked up Matthew's present (a box of

Disney characters) and headed up.

The smell of cooking on the fifth floor reminded me of a typical French granny's kitchen, where the saucepans are as big as mixing bowls. My heart pounding, I rang the bell. Marie opened the door. *This* was where that delicious smell was coming from. All of a sudden, I was ravenous. Marie led the way and I took off my shoes – a house rule – so I could walk on the rug.

I gazed at the floor in the living room where the table was laid. The Persian rug in the entrance hall flowed into more Persian rugs, drowning out the carpet underneath. There were medium-sized ones and big ones, like flower gardens.

Marie saw what I was looking at and said, 'These rugs were handmade, Lucy. When something's made by hand, it comes from the heart. The men and women who created these rugs wove their souls into them.'

The way she talked, I understood why we had to take our shoes off. It was about respect.

'With each new season,' Marie added, 'new patterns appear on the rugs. The patterns of those people living on the rugs. And so different lives come together . . .'

I turned to look at Matthew, who was already sitting at the table. He'd piled two cushions on top of each other on a chair, wedging him right up against the table. And he was clutching on to his spoon for dear life. When I said hello, there was no reaction from him. I looked at Marie.

'Eating is a key activity for Matthew,' she told me. 'It's 7.04p.m. by the clock on the video-player. Matthew recognises the numbers. He knows that supper's late . . .' She chuckled, but Matthew didn't join in.

'He always sits like that, by the way. Even if you try pushing him out a bit, he just tucks himself back in. It's like a bad habit. I think it makes him feel safe when he's all squashed up.'

Just then, Maougo appeared with a big soup tureen, and we moved to the table. Maougo and Marie were on either side of Matthew. I sat opposite him, while he stared at the tureen. Silently, Maougo got up and took our bowls.

'No beetroot for Matthew,' said Marie. 'No stock either.'

But Maougo knew exactly what to do and what not to do, in order to avoid triggering one of Matthew's tantrums. The soup was delicious. Nobody spoke. After a long silence broken only by clinking spoons, I said, 'It's very tasty!' and Maougo smiled at me.

'Maougo made it,' Marie explained, giving Maougo a friendly look. 'It's a recipe from her country.'

Matthew gobbled his soup. Sometimes he made snorting noises too. When he was full, he jumped down and tucked himself under the table. Neither of the two women seemed to mind about this. You'd think it was completely normal for him to crouch down like an animal. I braced myself. Was he going to start licking our feet? That's when I had a brainwave about François: of course, Matthew would make the perfect trainer to help François find his animal instincts again!

Matthew stayed on the carpet for the rest of the meal, and I almost forgot he was there, until he jumped towards the television, shouting, 'You turn it on, you turn it on, it's now!' He turned it on. A few seconds later, the weather forecast started.

I kept being surprised at how Matthew did things. The forecast started and he froze, but you could see all his senses were working overtime. It was like he was absorbing the information from all around him. If Martians ever invade Planet Earth in human form to swallow up our technology, I imagine they'd behave a bit like him.

Matthew looked like he'd been switched on by remote control. His whole body was straining towards the television, even his ears were twisted in its direction. And he was concentrating so hard, you'd think he'd made the rest of the world disappear – though not physically, of course, we're not made that way.

There was also something strange going on with his hands. He was holding them out in front of him, as if he was resting them on an invisible table. His fingers were spread wide and I could see their tips twitching. I was sure there was a transparent liquid flowing between him and the screen.

I looked round to see how the others were reacting. Marie had stopped eating, to tune into her son's wavelength. I don't think she'd turned into a statue because she was riveted by the weather forecast. I think she'd made herself disappear in order to help Matthew concentrate.

But Maougo's behaviour was another story. Before the forecast, we were about to try some sesame snaps drizzled with honey. Well, she just went right ahead and ate hers, without minding what anyone else was doing. So the world was split in two – like in *Sleeping Beauty* when everybody's frozen in a deep sleep, except for the fairies who are busy making sure the story has a happy ending. A spell had been cast over Matthew and Marie that didn't affect Maougo.

I was more and more curious about this woman from Russia.

At the end of the forecast, Matthew jumped up and shouted, 'You turn it off!' And he did. The session ended as abruptly as it had started. Matthew and Marie came back to life.

When we'd cleared the table, Marie signalled for me to follow her. We settled down in another corner of the living room, on a rug that was slightly different from the rest.

'It's a Russian rug,' Marie explained. 'The others are Persian. That kilim over there is Turkish, it's the only rug that's woven on a loom.'

I looked at the rug we were on. It was mostly aubergine-coloured with three orange and fuchsia pink diamonds in the middle. The closer in, the brighter the colours. I've got a Russian wooden babushka doll in my bedroom. The big doll hides a medium-sized doll which hides a smaller one, and so on until you get down to a doll so tiny it doesn't open up at all. I was lost in thought when Marie added, 'This is Maougo's favourite area. I don't know much about her past, but perhaps it reminds her of when she was young.'

Like a small spider, I wove a web with my thoughts. Maougo was a Russian doll. You could only see her outside layer at first, because she didn't talk. But little by little you got to know her on different levels, until you were close to her heart. The rug was a breakthrough, because it had given me a way in: I could see the colour of her memories.

Up until then, I hadn't been able to put my finger on what made that flat so special. But now I knew. It was very roomy, but full of nooks and crannies too. The rugs divided it up like hopscotch patterns, taking you to the four corners of the world. It was a home with lots of different spaces but no walls.

Maougo joined us with a tray, cups and a teapot. Matthew see-sawed behind her on tiptoes. The tea set was fancy, but the atmosphere was laid back. The Marottes and their piercing voices were a world away. We were in Russia, about to drink fennel tea. Matthew circled me like a bat, without bumping into me or looking at me either, as if he'd got his own radar system. Then, without warning, he flopped against me, his tummy on my back, and I didn't dare move in case he went away again. It was that time of evening when children want hugs. And Matthew was like a cat, the way he needed his.

The herbal tea tasted strange. Marie took two or three sips. Then came the moment I'd been waiting for. 'You want to know what autism is,' Marie began.

She didn't make it sound like a question, more like 'Once upon a time . . .', and we were off into another world. I tried to find the piece of paper with the definition on it in my pocket, without shifting about to much.

> **Autism (from the Greek, autos, oneself):**
> **pathological withdrawal into an interior**
> **world resulting in a loss of contact with**
> **reality and an inability to communicate**
> **with others.**

Matthew didn't seem to mind. He spread his hands through my hair in an army of fingers and, as Marie set us off on a journey, I could feel my bun falling out.

Marie: 'A psychoanalyst called Mr Bettelheim was the first person to turn his attention to autistic people. He called them fortresses, because they're trapped inside their own walls. Autistic people don't think the way we do and most of the time they don't talk either, they just make sounds. Communicating with them is very difficult. So is understanding them.'

'Like Maougo – she doesn't talk either.'

'No, Maougo doesn't speak French, but she can hold a conversation in Russian,' Marie answered. 'And not only that, but she's able to use other tools. She can communicate with gestures and looks. Autistic people are different, they're not open to other people, they withdraw into themselves. The world doesn't exist beyond them, it only exists inside them. They live alone deep inside their beings, in a space we don't know about.'

I was struggling to understand. Marie pointed to the mobile of tortoises encrusted with tiny mirrors. 'Matthew,' she explained, 'can spend hours navigating those reflections.'

Marie talked and Matthew made loops in my hair. I surrendered my head to him, lock by lock. I didn't want him to stop. Instead of letting me stroke him this special cat was stroking me . . .

'You see,' Marie went on, 'life on earth is about looking at each other, in the same way that the earth moves round the sun. That's how the solar system works. But autistic people are like small independent planets that have landed here by chance, and instead of looking at the other earthlings as they move around them, they spin inside themselves. So they become their own planetary systems, and reaching them is as difficult as getting on a merry-go-round when it's already moving.'

'But Matthew talks!'

'He does,' Marie agreed, 'but if you listen carefully you'll realise he's talking to himself. He cradles himself with words that fly off.'

'That's not true!' I butted in, reminding her of Matthew's words before the weather forecast. 'He said, "It's now, you turn it on!" He was calling you!'

'I don't think so, Lucy,' Marie disagreed. 'When I'm talking to him, I might say "Matthew, can you come here?" By his own special kind of logic, he's called "you". So "you turn it on" means "Matthew turn it on". Very occasionally, I've seen him talking to his teddy bear. He might say something like "I'm coming, pumpkin!" and he'll move his toy towards him. "I" means the other person and "you" means Matthew . . . It makes sense if you look at it from a certain angle. When I'm talking to him about me, I say "I" to him, so "I" means other people. And when other people are talking to him, they say "you". So "you" means him. There's a different kind of logic to his code.'

All right, I accepted he was talking to himself. 'But sometimes he looks at us!' I pointed out. And just to convince myself, I added, 'I mean, he's like Maougo: he talks with his eyes.'

Marie agreed, but she needed to explain a bit more. 'He used to stare blankly at things before, or else he was seeing something we couldn't. Now, he can focus on real objects and not keep disappearing into the make-believe world of his dreams. He can focus on the television or the computer, but they're not living beings. And it's not a form of communication. Later on . . . Later on, perhaps . . . With a lot of love . . .'

Marie looked away and I started thinking out loud, 'But Marie . . . if he can give things names, even if he's talking to himself, it means he's been listening . . .'

'Yes, Lucy. That's why we live in hope.'

'Hurray! And you know what else? He communicates with his hands. He's stroking me.'

'He's been stroking you for a long time,'

Marie replied, 'and he keeps on making the same movements, as if the record's scratched and he's got stuck in the groove.'

'But I like it.'

'Me too. But what you have to realise is he's clinging to your hair. He's holding on. By stroking you, he's stroking himself, which makes him feel less scared. But he'll have to grow up. One day, he's got to become a man. If he just repeats the same gestures *ad infinitum*, he'll keep going round and round in circles. It stops him seeing. It's the opposite of making progress.'

When Marie had finished, I wanted to cry.

It was after ten o'clock when I headed back down to our flat. What with the rugs from all over the globe and so many different interior worlds, I felt there were lots of different atmospheres floating around inside me. Mum wanted to know how it went, but I didn't say much. I was on MY OWN planet and I didn't want to communicate any more. In my bedroom, under my mezzanine bed, I drew two flags. The Russian flag was for Maougo and in the left-hand corner of the French flag, I wrote M for Marie.

Chapter 5

My silence lasted all night – the only time I'm quiet is when I'm asleep. But as soon as I woke up, I blurted out the whole story: the weather forecast, Maougo talking with her eyes, the fortress, eyes that couldn't focus properly, musical words, the tortoise mobile, the solar system, eyes that saw things in mirrors . . .

My parents were stunned, and I thought they'd understood what was at stake. 'There you go,' I said, keen to hear what they had to say.

But instead of following my lead, they let me down. Big time.

Dad sounded annoyed. 'What kind of crazy ideas are they putting into her head? Eyes that can't focus seeing things in mirrors!'

Mum hadn't been listening to Dad anyway. 'So tell me . . .' (Asking a question was a positive sign, or so I thought.) 'So tell me,' she said again, 'what did you have to eat?'

I ask you. There I was, explaining about a little boy nobody understands. About how the things he sees with his eyes are so different from what we see with ours, that we don't have any words to describe them. I was telling them how he's so scared of gaps, he has to squash himself in between the table and his chair. I was explaining how clinging to people's hair makes him feel safe. And all they could say was, 'What kind of crazy ideas are they putting into her head?' On top of which, Mum was up to her old trick of judging people by what they ate.

I got up and stormed out in disgust, because sometimes you've got to make a stand. But being a chatterbox, I couldn't help staging a comeback. 'We had borsch, Mum. It's Russian and it's delicious. It's a perfect blend of proteins, vitamins and fibre, with a spoonful of yoghurt for the calcium quota. What you'd call a square meal.'

That put a cork in it.

Later on, in my bedroom, I got out my dictionary.

> **To communicate: transmit; reveal; share.**
> **To be joined by a passage.**

Marie's words were going round in my head: 'Matthew can make contact with things, but not people ... One day, perhaps ... With a lot of love . . .' And that was when it hit me. I wasn't interested in getting to know everyone in our building any more. I just wanted to get to know Matthew.

The next day was Sunday, so François was

coming round. Theo and I had organised for Matthew to join us on our walk. Marie had spoken to him about it, because Matthew hates surprises. She'd also insisted on one thing: we mustn't let go of his hand, apart from when we were inside.

François arrived. We went up to the fifth floor and rang at the agreed time. Matthew was ready and waiting behind the door. We set off. Theo met us in front of Père-Lachaise Cemetery. Dogs aren't allowed in the cemetery so, a few metres before we got there, I signalled to François to jump into my bag – but I never let go of Matthew's hand.

François lives in the posh part of Paris so he's used to this kind of transport, although his normal travelling bag is much more chic. It all went smoothly. We made it through the entrance under the gatekeeper's nose. I pretended butter wouldn't melt in my mouth, Theo smiled infectiously, François was hiding in my bag, and Matthew see-sawed along. What we didn't realise was that Maougo was following behind, in case things got out of hand.

It was autumn and the earth smelled damp. We kept to the main path for a little way, before turning off into the area of the cemetery where the really old gravestones are. There was less chance of being caught there – people who've been dead a long time don't get as many visitors as the newly dead. A carpet of leaves scrunched under our feet and Matthew jumped from grave to grave. When we thought we were out of danger, I half-opened François' bag and he poked a frightened head out. François had more of a sense of what was taboo than Matthew. Theo threw a stick – something dogs can't resist. François jumped out of the bag. Then Matthew jumped up as well and a furious chase followed. Matthew and François grabbed the stick and rolled on the ground, sending the leaves flying. Who was dragging and who was being dragged? I couldn't tell. But a mini-cyclone swooped down on our part of the cemetery. It was a sweet, crazy sight. Matthew and François even looked like each other.

Further off, silent as a Native American on a trail, Maougo stood watching us.

I'd love to have seen the look on her face when Theo and I joined in the dance too. Did she start spinning as well? Craziness can be catching! Then again, maybe we weren't crazy. Maybe we were just deliriously happy.

We were all tangled up. Theo laughed like a stream. I felt like a tree: my arms had turned into branches and my fingers were the leaves. The more I spun, the closer I got to the sky. We were systems that wouldn't be tamed. We were the kings of the world. We were autistic!

Suddenly, Matthew started shouting, 'You're crying! You're crying!' Using Marie's logic, I translated this to mean 'I'm crying! I'm crying!' I realised Matthew was being autumn. He was being the falling leaves. Matthew made the small leap from autumn to the weather forecast, and climbed on to a cross. 'Good evening and welcome!'

I stopped. He sounded just like a television presenter. He was standing straight and serious, looking very grown-up. A presenter on a stone cross, announcing the weather forecast. He was spot-on. He divided France in two, north and south of the Loire river. I don't know how he did it, but as he was describing the weather his body seemed to become a map and he pointed to bits of it. It was amazing. Then at the end he sang the theme music. We could hear the sound and see the images: it was happening for real. So real, in fact, that suddenly, without warning, Matthew fell in . . .

We had to get back because of François. We were allowed out until five o'clock, and we needed to be punctual. We didn't want our parents getting suspicious. But when the time came to leave, there was no getting through to Matthew. He'd locked himself inside his television set and thrown away the keys. Theo and I took him by the hand. We tried everything, pushing and pulling him like maniacs. But Matthew lifted his arms and started singing advertising jingles, then he threw himself to the ground and spun around. Every bit of his body was a television set and nothing was going to persuade him to turn back into Matthew again.

I was worried and started getting annoyed. Even Theo was fed up. Only François stayed calm.

Matthew just kept on spinning. Panic stations. Père-Lachaise is normally so peaceful, but suddenly it turned back into a cemetery, full of shrieking spirits and ghosts and scary things that make you want to run away. We begged, we bargained, we promised . . . We didn't know which saint to call on, when . . . Maougo appeared.

Where had she come from? How did she know about stuff spiralling out of control? It didn't matter. We were so happy to see her, we didn't bother asking any questions. There she was, a big woman with a calm aura, and I immediately felt safe. I knew she'd change everything with a simple gesture, like she'd done that day in front of the lift.

Theo and I edged back to make room for her. Matthew was still spinning. Maougo moved forward with her head at an angle. She swayed gently as she started singing the same tune in synch with Matthew. A voice that doesn't speak is an incredible instrument when it starts humming. Matthew slowed down to let her climb on, because she'd understood his merry-go-round. But instead of joining him, she kept her body stiff as a post and gently took his hand, guiding him to her hair. Then she freed him from the whirlwind, as if she was using a piece of rope to pull him out. It was a miracle. I looked at Theo. She was blown away too, and it suddenly made sense why women have long hair.

That evening, Theo and I talked it over. It was time for a re-cap.

François had breezed through the checkpoint

again with flying colours. He was on a roll after the wind, the autumn smells, and skidding around in the leaves. And he hadn't panicked in the face of the shouting whirlwind. He was definitely starting to behave more like a real dog.

As for Matthew, he'd followed us without any more fuss, which was just as well. But we'd nearly lost him in his interior world. We'd got some work to do on our rescue techniques.

I asked my parents for a new notebook, so we could write down some of our observations. Dad frowned. You'd think he preferred me not to use my brain. But since he couldn't come up with any reason why not, he produced a notebook.

We'd got two missions: putting meaning back into François' life and saving Matthew from drowning. From now on, Friday evenings and Sundays were days for experimenting. And as it happened, my parents were going out the following Friday, so I was spending the night at Marie's.

I'd already slept under the stars. But not even the most beautiful night sky over the highest mountains could compare with what was about to happen.

It was late, eleven o'clock. Marie switched off the big Japanese ball that looked like the sun and turned on a little lamp. It gave off a softer glow, like the moon. And in its hazy light, she sat at the table and wrote her diary.

Maougo got up and appeared like a giant statue by the window, making time stand still. Her solid frame was preparing the peaceful night ahead.

As for Matthew, he sat on the angel rug, which is called that because there's a little terracotta angel overhanging it, nailed to the side of a bookshelf. There are also two coloured glass jars on one of the shelves. The blue one's for evenings, and the yellow one's for mornings. Matthew grabbed the blue jar and sat down in front of the angel. He even looked like it when he bent his head down. The only difference was that *his* wings were folded. His hand dived in and came back out again full of marbles. He dropped them like bombs, in a kind of song. The day marbles were glass, but the night marbles were cotton wool covered in foil. Lurking in the shadow, the marbles caught the light and sparkled. Matthew was concentrating so hard his eyes looked silver too. The drip-drip turned into rain. A rain of stars that lit up in his eyes.

Marie had finished. She closed her diary, got up and turned out the desk light. This switched off the little silver marbles, creating a blanket of silence. Maougo moved away from the French windows. Matthew put the blue jar back next to the yellow one and see-sawed to his bed where he buried himself up to his chin. Marie started the tape of songs to make him feel drowsy. The tape unwinds sleep. Without it, Matthew would never drop off. Finally, Marie went into her own bedroom and Maougo settled down on the landing floor outside Matthew's door. She turned the tape over and over, as patiently as an angel, until he fell asleep.

Matthew only drifts off when the night is full of songs.

I found myself all alone in the sitting room. I opened my notebook, like an imp in the heart of the slumbering night:

Friday evening, 10 October

It was hard putting the magic of a silent scene into words. I'd seen something like soundless poetry. I wrote,

Up on the fifth floor, under the roof, Matthew eats stars as he goes to sleep . . .

Then I wrote a long detailed account, and at the end I put,

Marbles tumble through the night, like stars of sleep in his eyes.

But writing about things doesn't always mean you understand them. Something was still bothering me: who *was* Maougo? The next day,

Theo and I had a discussion about her.

'What's she got that we haven't that lets her understand Matthew?' Theo wanted to know.

The more we mulled it over, the more one answer sprang to mind: she didn't talk. Perhaps you had to be wordless to understand silence, like blind people seeing with their hands. We decided she and Matthew were linked at the heart. Hearts have their own wavelengths. And when she let Matthew play with her straight blonde hair, that hair became a bridge that filled the gap between them. Matthew held on to it the way you'd cling to a princess's hair in a fairy story, when you'd got to get out of the labyrinth to escape the evil monster.

So we decided there were two possible explanations. Either Maougo was a fairy in disguise, hiding under her blonde hair, or her past life had made her so wise that now she understood everything.

chapter 6

The following Friday, Theo and I were walking across the square. We ran into Matthew, who was taking a biscuit for a walk. It was raining. We were amazed, firstly because it was the kind of weather for staying indoors, and secondly because Matthew was treating the biscuit like a king. Under the damp song of the sky, sheltered by an arbour, Marie told us a story.

That night, Theo couldn't sleep. Too many thoughts buzzing around inside her head. Both her little sisters were fast asleep on a duvet next to her. Eight-year-old Suleiman was stretching an elastic band to snapping point on a mattress joined to Theo's bed. In the end, Theo sat up. She'd borrowed the journal from me. She opened it and started writing, by the light of the street lamp filtering in through the window.

Friday evening, 17 October
Matthew likes petit-beurre biscuits so much he doesn't eat them. If you give him one, he takes it for a walk, he lets it breathe, he fingers its edges. He uses it to stroke his cheek and never lets go. So it's like he's lost an arm, because he's only got one free hand – the other one's holding the biscuit – and everything's tricky. If it rains, he protects the biscuit. If he walks in a puddle, he holds it at arm's length. This can last all morning, until something happens and the biscuit crumbles. Matthew tries sticking the broken bits back together again, but it's no good. He cries like his heart's been broken and nothing can cheer him up, not even another biscuit. In the end he eats the crumbs, even if it's just to get

rid of them. And he starts to feel better because the biscuit tastes so delicious.

When Theo looked up, she noticed Mamassa's duvet had come off. She got up quietly, tucked her sister's plump little body back inside the warmth, and picked up the thread of her thoughts again.

When he was a baby, Matthew used to scream and spin and shout. But he only cried twice. Both times have stuck in Marie's memory.

The first, Matthew was six months old. It was before they knew Maougo. Matthew had gone to sleep under the tortoise mobile, his eyes lost in its mirrors. There was a song playing on the radio. Suddenly, something made Marie look at her son. His eyes had filled with tears.

'I picked him up,' Marie told us, 'weeping and wet and silent. But he didn't seem to be hungry or in pain. He never cried because he was hungry or in pain . . .'

That's when a friend of Marie's said, 'It's the

song, can you see how he's listening to it?' And sure enough, when the song had finished, Matthew calmed down and went back to his tortoises.

'I used to think,' Marie added, 'that babies only cried if they wanted to eat or be held. But Matthew was crying out of pure emotion.'

That evening, for the first time, Marie realised her son was special. She had the King of Hearts in her family.

Suleiman was asleep too now and the bedroom was purring with the sounds of drowsy breathing, but Theo carried on . . .

The second time he cried, he'd just broken his glass bottle. Marie lined up all the other bottles to show him it didn't matter. She even went downstairs to the chemist's to buy him a new bottle – just like the one that had got broken. But it was no good. His eyes kept streaming with tears. New things could never replace old things for him. That's true love for you. He was so upset, he went on hunger strike after he'd stopped crying. No more sounds and no more

food. He wanted to die out of solidarity for his
broken bottle. Two days later, he fainted from
hunger. He ended up in hospital.

'D'you realise,' Theo asked me the next day, handing back the journal, 'D'you realise how much he feels things? He's not just being sympathetic, he really takes on the pain of the other person.'

'You said it,' I told her, 'he can feel *things* but not people. So it's not about sympathy and it's certainly not about communication.'

Theo doesn't normally get annoyed, but she did this time. 'OK, so he doesn't communicate. But he can become a biscuit or a bottle, he gets into things. D'you remember at Père-Lachaise how he shouted, "You're crying, you're crying!" because *he* was the one who was crying. It's crazy, isn't it?'

My doubts held me back at first, but by the end of the day her belief had taken hold of me like a bug. I was hatching something. You've got to listen to your instincts. Sometimes, truth is

stranger than make-believe. I was at fever pitch
by the evening. I got up, I had to write it all
down. It was the middle of the night again, and
I was buried in our logbook.

A fairy lives at 11 Rue Merlin. You can only see her with your
heart because she's not particularly pretty. There's also a
little boy who's not like anybody you've ever met because he's
his own system.

The more I wrote the clearer it was. Of course,
it was staring me in the face. Matthew was
different from us. He was a cosmic being. An
extraterrestrial with special powers that let him
turn into whatever he was looking at, whatever
he touched, whatever he listened to or smelled.

My biro was running away with me:

Matthew: a chameleon with a heart made of modelling clay
or Plasticine.

Logically, this was where all our conclusions had

been leading. In my head I went over that first supper again, when he turned on the television. He was like a sponge soaking up the weather forecast. I thought back to the *petit-beurre* biscuits and the song on the radio when he could feel the singer's emotions. I could see it raining leaves again, raining silver marbles that disappeared inside his eyes. Now I understood the drawing on his front door: a little boy with elephant ears and hands like wings. Matthew had drawn himself, it was a self-portrait. A little boy who heard everything and could fly away.

I was onto something: Matthew was still a child, a junior extraterrestrial, an apprentice right at the beginning of his training. For the time being, he was learning how to turn himself into things, because it was easier and he didn't have to think about it too much. But I wrote,

One day he'll start turning into people. And it won't just be about communication, it'll be total fusion. He'll be better than us.

What a hero! It was all I could do to stop myself running up to the fifth floor. Talk about a revelation: this was a real encounter of the third kind. But a voice of reason held me back. It was too important to be announced in a rush. There are lots of doubters in the world who'd think I was crazy if I shouted out the news. I'd got to find a proper way of explaining it.

CHAPTER 7

When I looked out of my window the next day I could see Theo on the pavement below. It was Sunday, so I had a ready-made excuse to pop out: getting the baguette for breakfast. My parents don't like me hanging about outside. They say things like 'the street paves the way to prison'. I called out to Theo to wait for me and I ran down. I put my arm around her to test out my theory about an encounter of the third kind confidentially.

Before I'd finished, she butted in, 'Of course, Matthew's a wizard.'

Extraterrestrial or wizard, same thing. I was irritated at first, because she'd interrupted before I'd got to the best bit. But then I changed my mind: it was going to take at least two of us to get our idea accepted.

'Go on, read out the definition again,' she said.

I fumbled around in my pocket, looking for the piece of paper, and refreshed her memory,

> **Autism: Pathological withdrawal into an interior world resulting in a loss of contact with reality and an inability to communicate with others.**

A heated debate followed. In the end, we agreed it should say,

> **Autism: Unusual withdrawal into an interior world resulting from such a strong contact with reality that people can become objects.**

We shook hands. We were together on this.

But if we wanted to challenge a dictionary definition, we'd got our work cut out . . . I wasn't sure we'd make it.

Mum pointed out I'd taken my time buying the baguette again.

That afternoon, Theo and I went up to the fifth floor. It was Matthew's birthday and Marie was taking us to see an African dance show.

Matthew doesn't like surprises, so he was very restless. There were three taps backstage before the curtain rose on a tree trunk with a child beating out a rhythm on it with his stick. Matthew slipped away from Maougo and headed down to the stage, as if he'd been called. To our amazement, he positioned himself under the raised platform where he started moving. He copied the child, hitting his own imaginary tree trunk, and the music took over. It unleashed him. There were two performances now: one on stage where a black child was wearing white, and another in the auditorium where a white child was wearing green. The music swelled. The stage was filled with percussion instruments, from djembes to balaphones. Matthew was brilliant. He was communicating via the universal language of music. There was a standing ovation and lots of cheering. It was a hit! The actors acknowledged Matthew. Marie cried, Maougo smiled, Matthew giggled. Theo and I looked at each other: this kid was really special.

The next day, Theo and I replayed the scene a thousand times. 'Matthew's found a language. It's called hand-music. That's how we've got to talk to him.' It didn't sound such a big deal when you put it like that, but we'd come a long way in those three sentences.

'Matthew isn't really a fortress,' said Theo. 'He communicates with and against things.' Then she got really excited. 'Let's take him back to my house after school. Grandpa plays the tama, which is a sort of drum. You hold it in the crook of your arm,' she explained. 'In the bush, they use it instead of a telephone.'

When class was over, we headed straight to

Matthew's, and he agreed to come with us. Grandpa Balthazar was always up for talking about things at Theo's house.

'Hello little brother,' he greeted Matthew.

Matthew didn't react until he noticed the tama, and then he stretched out his arm.

Grandpa Balthazar got there before him and hit it.

'That's me saying hello. Hello! Hello!'

Fatoumata and Mamassa crawled over, attracted by the noise.

Balthazar started beating out different sounds – once, twice – Matthew stretched out his hands, Balthazar passed him the tama, Matthew copied the sounds. They got increasingly complicated, longer and longer, more and more elaborate, but Matthew kept on copying them. He didn't always get it right first time. But he started over and over again until it was perfect.

It was a game to begin with. Grandpa's eyes were laughing. Without giving anything away, Matthew's were listening. Then something changed in the way they were looking at each other. Matthew was completely focused on Balthazar – especially Balthazar's hands – and Balthazar only had eyes for Matthew. Theo, the girls and I barely existed now. It was all happening between Grandpa and Matthew. Age and size didn't count any more, sounds were all that mattered. Grandpa's hands were as agile as when he was a young man and Matthew looked like the drawing on his front door: a little boy with big ears and hands like wings.

That evening, we took Matthew back home with the tama tucked under his arm. When he walked through his front door and saw Marie, he beat out the sounds for 'Hello!'

> Hello: term of salutation.
>
> Salutation: show of civility through gesture or word, made on meeting somebody.

I'll eat my hat if that's not communication.

CHAPTER • 8

Let's leave the autumn behind and head into winter. One December evening, there was a ring at the door. It was the Marottes and I had a sneaky feeling it was serious. It wasn't a Sunday and they weren't the kind of people to change their routine unless something was up. Mrs Marotte looked very white. And François wasn't being carried like a nincompoop in that shopping bag. For once, they'd let him walk.

The sound of that squeaky voice made Mum

appear and Mrs Marotte collapsed into her arms, all sirens wailing. Mr Marotte stayed on the landing, stiff as a poker. Only François wandered in looking relaxed. He went into the sitting room and settled under the window. I stayed in the hall trying to work out what was going on. I wasn't just curious, I was completely baffled by what was behind this strange behaviour. It turned out somebody had died, and François would be in the way. The Marottes wanted to put him in kennels . . . They had me scared, but only for a second because they added 'with you', as in *with us*. They wanted to put François in kennels in OUR FLAT! My heart skipped a beat. 'Wicked!' Three faces stared at me. OK, it was bad timing, so I babbled, 'What I mean is, I'm glad François is coming to stay with us.' And I backed out of the hall, in a rush to get myself out of the hole I'd just dug.

François hadn't moved from the window, where he looked as Zen as a wise old prophet. He was a sly one. The week before, he'd had his nose in every dustbin and been chasing all the pigeons . . . We'd made a lot of progress since his lap-dog days. I gave him a hug. I hoped the Marottes really would leave him with us. A tiny twitch in his neck told me what he was thinking. 'Don't worry. I'm here to stay.' And when Mrs Marotte swooped down on him, covering him with kisses, I knew we'd won.

Once the Marottes had gone, the flat was calm again and there was a warm glow inside me. Mum had been caught off-guard, unable to say no to a friend in floods of tears. François didn't know what to do with his new-found freedom. And I wasn't sure if I was coming or going: I'd given up on the idea of having a pet ages ago, even a microscopic one, because Mum was so against it . . .

'Well, there we are!' I said after a while. To show I'd got the situation under control, I grabbed the wicker basket. 'Can I put this in my bedroom, Mum?'

There was no question of François sleeping in the sitting room, or in my parents' bedroom or in the kitchen, and even less chance of him trotting up and down the landing with those little paws of his, so she agreed. Yes! François jumped into the basket and we made a triumphant exit, me carrying the basket high above my head and François on top, a victory mascot.

François coming to stay at our flat marked a new era which, as luck would have it, fitted in with the Christmas holidays.

> **Era: An epoch in which a new order of things is established.**

Mum and Dad were working and Granny couldn't cope with the idea of a dog at her place, but someone had to look after François. So the first morning, after tons of warnings, I was given my own key to the flat so I could take François out for walks. My face didn't give anything away, but inside me each molecule of my body was jumping up and down. No more excuses when I wanted to go out. Freedom and the open road were ours at last.

As soon as my parents had gone, I summoned Theo. 'Meeting at my place in an hour!' One hour later, she got here. We headed up to find Matthew, like two queens with their lion (I'd always dreamed about the king of the jungle, after Joseph Kessel's *The Lion*).

Marie wasn't sure. 'Matthew doesn't like surprises.'

But François barked and Matthew rushed over and put on his shoes in a flash. An astonished smile spread across Marie's face. Maougo smiled too in the background, but it was a different kind of smile, as if she already knew . . .

We were off. The lift went down. Our excitement climbed. François pawed the ground, and so did Matthew. The door opened, Matthew jumped out. Matthew, the free spirit, Matthew no holds barred. We formed a line. A black hand in a white hand in a little white hand that see-sawed along, and a mad dog running ahead. A long way back, bringing up the rear like a heavy fire door, was a stocky figure you might not have realised was part of our group. Maougo didn't try hiding the fact she was there any more, she just kept her distance and didn't get involved, so was no bother to us. We didn't feel like were being watched, but it was reassuring to know nothing could happen to us. Half-open courtyards, hidden nooks and crannies, dead-ends and shortcuts. We pretended the edge of the pavement was a tightrope, we jumped the puddles, we skimmed the edge of the grass. Even Theo, who spends a lot of time outdoors, saw another side to things. This is how you get to know a place like the back of your hand. You head off-piste, you go round and about, you walk on walls. Suddenly, Matthew dived into a café and Theo was so surprised she let go. But Marie had insisted on one golden rule: always hold each other by the hand apart from when we were inside, and even then only if we were all together. A long way behind us, Maougo hadn't left her lookout post. We didn't know what we were letting ourselves in for, but we went in.

* * *

The barman was the only person there, and Matthew sat down in his squashy kind of way. He was tired of running and he'd noticed that café chairs were made for sitting on. But ideas like customers, money and ordering things had completely passed him by. There was trouble ahead. Theo and I were both stumped. We stood back, like spectators, just in case there was a happy ending. But disaster was guaranteed with Matthew.

The barman came over.

'What can I do for you, young man?'

Matthew had a faraway look in his eyes as he pointed a threatening finger at the man.

'When you're sixteen years old,' he prophesied, 'you'll prick your finger on the sharp end of a rifle, and you'll die from it . . .' And he was off in fits of diabolical laughter.

How were we going to get out of this? Theo was the first to react. 'We're really sorry, but Matthew's a bit strange you see . . .'

'He's autistic, but he's a great kid,' I explained.

'He's tired because we've been walking for a long time. He just wants to sit down . . .'

My turn again: 'But the thing is we haven't got any money with us.'

Back to Theo (you feel more confident when there are two of you talking), 'We won't stay long . . .'

'If we drag him outside, he won't understand, because he's not doing anything wrong.'

'And then he might throw a tantrum.'

I glanced over at the table. Matthew was still squashed up and François was lying at his feet. 'His tantrums are like whirlwinds. They drown him, and even though we've got long hair we don't know how to fish him back out again yet.'

Theo flashed one of her sparkling smiles: 'Please . . .'

The suspense lasted a couple of seconds, and it was almost unbearable. Two seconds is a long time when you've got the black dragon of a tantrum snarling on the horizon. Then the barman smiled and pointed to the table. 'What can I get you?' he asked, rubbing his hands.

Theo sat down triumphantly. 'Coca-Cola!'

'An Orangina, please,' I asked, more quietly.

'And what about the little boy?' inquired the barman, looking at Matthew.

I was ready for that. 'Just a glass of water for Matthew, please. He's not being punished or anything, but his mum told us he only drinks water. Coloured drinks look like paints to Matthew, so they'd taste horrible.'

The scene ended with François wagging his tail as he lapped up the water in his bowl.

It was the same story the following day: my parents left and Theo arrived. We ran up to get Matthew, and he followed us or, to be more accurate, went ahead while Maougo trailed behind.

By eleven o'clock we were in another café, where a woman with long hair was sitting minding her own business. Matthew spotted her as he walked past the café and all of a sudden he braked, opened the door, rushed at her and buried his hands in her hair. The woman jumped up and let out a piercing shriek. I gritted my teeth. How embarrassing! But Matthew launched a second attack, even scarier than the first, and started making his '*fsshhtt!*' sound effects. Theo and I looked at each other and burst out laughing . . . Then came the final straw: François got overexcited and jumped on the poor woman too.

Given the scale of the disaster, I had to say something. 'I'm *sooo* sorry!'

'Right, that's enough now,' the barman cut in. 'Leave the lady in peace!'

'He's autistic,' I objected, 'he likes long hair, it's his way of making contact with people.'

The barman muttered the usual stuff about children being badly brought up these days. Theo was about to lose her temper. Luckily, the lady stepped in. She stuck up for Matthew. Maybe, inside every woman, there's a maternal streak. 'Leave it, he's very sweet,' she said, 'he's not bothering me.' But she tried to smooth her hair back down all the same.

So Theo took the stage and told the shouting whirlwind story, the one where Matthew gets more and more wound up in his circles and starts shouting, and Maougo comes to the rescue with her long hair. That clinched it! The lady was touched by how big the little boy's troubles were. She was even flattered that he found her long hair comforting. It made her feel like a fairy godmother . . . She held out her hair to Matthew and sat him on her knees.

'Drinks are on me,' she said gently.

Another happy ending with Coca-Cola, Orangina, a glass of water and a bowl for the dog.

chapter 9

We were making lightning progress on those daily walks. I'd given up on the idea of getting to know everyone in our block of flats, but I was getting to know the world.

François had taken a leaf out of Matthew's book by starting to lay on the charm. He'd learnt to beg for things and sometimes even to steal them. He was just messing around, but he was also learning about dodging, escaping and running till he was out of breath. He was finding out about forbidden fruit and weighing up the risks: fun and risk often go hand in hand. He'd become friends with all the butchers and he teased the local top dogs. We went everywhere, running like lunatics to defend his bits of steak. He'd taken over all the earthy patches to bury his treasure. A prouder dog never stomped his territory.

Around that time, I decided I want to redecorate my bedroom, as if I was re-making the world. So I asked for a few bits and bobs. Dad started ranting.

I tried explaining: 'I won't make any holes in the walls, I just need scissors and tape . . .' But I ended up triggering a family row.

Dad's always been a stickler for the rules. 'Have you taken complete leave of your senses? *The tenant is responsible for any damage to the property*, article thingamyjig of the Civil Code. And, article 1384, *I'm responsible for you and your actions until you're eighteen*. So you can shelve your idea of a bedroom makeover, and we'll talk about it again in six years' time.'

'Her bedroom *is* her own space,' Mum piped up. 'We all need a place we can call our own.'

Dad was shouting and Mum was crying, but since it was time for both of them to go to work, I ended up in my bedroom with a pair of old scissors and a roll of tape. I had a sneaky feeling I should be keeping a 'logbook' about my parents' behaviour!

While I was waiting for Theo, I dug out the pile of women's magazines from under my bed. Theo's mum collects magazines people leave by recycling bins, to read them with her friends. You get two kinds of recipes inside: how to make tasty food and how to stay pretty. Theo joined me and we started tearing stuff out.

We wanted to make two piles: natural landscapes on the right, everything else on the left. When we'd done that, we chucked everything else away and spread out the landscapes. Sunsets, snow that never melts, stretches of desert, seas, the flightpaths of wild geese, icebergs, autumn colours, sunny skies, starry skies, moons . . . My carpet had disappeared. Singing at the tops of our voices, we cut things out and covered a section of wall so that, moving from left to right, you left the snow that never melted and headed down towards the high plateaux, before passing through forests, mountain streams and waterfalls pouring into frozen seas. Then, gradually, the seas warmed up and became turquoise. You reached a fine sandy beach that turned into a desert and then an oasis. It was never-ending, because the last things you saw were three dots . . . like the line on the horizon you can never reach.

Those were the pictures sorted. Next for the words.

I fancied painting great big sentences across the walls . . . But with a dad like mine, it wasn't even worth thinking about. So we wondered about Marie's computer instead, the one that makes a two-dimensional picture stand up and become a 3D body with breasts and hips and a back when the character turns round; it even

makes the wind move in her hair. All you have to
do is click. It looks completely realistic from
every angle. Theo and I agreed that if our
sentences came out of that computer, they'd be
truer, clearer and more stylish. So up we went.
Marie was fine about it. She woke the machine
with the flick of a switch and when the box
started humming she left us, closing the door
behind her. We needed to concentrate on the
task ahead.

We'd brought two books with us, and we
took it in turns to type. We chose a font called
'Avant-garde' and a 3D style, as well as making
the letters as big as they'd go. We could fit one
word onto each page. When we'd finished, we
went back down with a heap of pages and our
arms felt weighed down with truths. Back in
my bedroom, François was over the moon
about the pictures. My bedroom door didn't
shut the world out any more, it opened
onto it.

By four o'clock, there was a banner hanging from the ceiling.

YOU ONLY SEE WITH YOUR HEART, BECAUSE YOUR EYES MISS WHAT MATTERS.

There was a dialogue on the door . . .

'One only understand the things that one tames,' said the fox.

'What must I do to tame you?' asked the little prince.

The fox recommended patience.

On François' side of the room, *The Call of the Wild* rang out. It was an extract from Jack London's book, which we read at school last year. *Obeying the call, he would spring to his feet and dash away, and on and on, for hours, under the cool canopy of the forest* . . . To illustrate it, we'd painted a handsome dog standing in a snow-covered plain, with the caption, *The pack of wolves poured into the clearing; and in the centre*

stood Buck, *motionless as a statue, waiting for them.*
François can't read, of course, but we'll tell him
the story often enough. And once the evening
wind gets into the ventilation system, he'll end
up believing it.

The final touch involved scattering words on
their own, here and there. Like *communication,
look, smile, freedom, cock's crow, blue, hair, hope* and
battle. We talked a lot about that last word. We
didn't mean war. We meant fighting for love,
fighting to grow up. But we'd stuck it up
without any explanation, to make you think
about it for yourself. Finally, we added *trust*
and *courage.*

It was a total makeover. Theo and I stepped
back to get a better view. It looked perfect to
us. Theo suggested we get her grandfather to
see it.

'Balthazar's great for giving advice, because
he's so old he's wise and crazy at the same time.'

We went to find him and he followed us
back saying: 'It'd be my pleasure, young ladies,
and a great honour too.' (Balthazar's sentences

are often slow, but his timing's always right.) Balthazar walked through the door, cast his eye around, and sat down to stop himself from falling over. When he found his voice again, he beat out a gigantic rhythm on the bed frame. Wow, it was like a cockerel crowing to wake the sun. Matthew should have been here. Then Balthazar spoke, but using words this time, 'It's extraordinary! Goodness me, I've got two young artists here! But listen . . . there's something missing . . . (he went quiet). Can you hear? (he was quiet again) . . . It's the sound of the earth, the sound of the trees, the noises of the little animals, the sea breathing . . . THE MUSIC! What's missing here is the music of the world.'

And then he stood up purposefully. 'Come back to my den,' he said, 'I've got just what you need.'

We set off with a great fanfare. Balthazar led the way. At 7 Rue Merlin, we walked through the front door, which might as well not be there because it's always open. Balthazar disappeared and came back with a tape that had 'The Sound of Earth' written on it. Without saying a word, he closed the shutters and plunged us into complete darkness . . . We couldn't hear anything to start with. Then we made out cracklings, rustling wings and animal cries.

'You could have heard these sounds at the dawn of our planet,' whispered Balthazar, 'before mankind appeared.'

Then the sounds of human evolution started up. First came fire, then a wheel over stony ground, the Iron Age, the telegraph and lots of other stuff . . . Next, there were greetings in different languages as well as different kinds of music from all over the world. Finally, we were on the ocean floor with whales singing in the big blue. When the tape went quiet, we opened the shutters again.

'All these sounds,' Balthazar explained, 'were recorded on to a golden disc that was put inside a space capsule headed for the stars, in search of other civilisations that might exist out there. The scientists' aim was for mankind to introduce itself, together with everything that's wonderful about the earth. So it's a love letter to outer space.'

A cosmic silence followed. Then Balthazar picked up again . . .

'Maybe nobody will ever find this message. Maybe it'll never be decoded. Maybe they won't understand our words but they'll be able to hear our emotions through our music. We have no way of knowing . . . But what matters is trying.'

By the end of the day, I was wrapped in my thoughts. First, I'd discovered internal worlds. Now an outside world was opening up to me, a world where love had set off in a rocket in a woosh of communication. Communicating with Matthew was a similar struggle, and we'd taken the route of music. So we were on the right track.

When my parents got back home from work, my bedroom was under the ocean. I'd got no idea what they thought, because all I could hear was the whale song travelling through the deepest waters . . . Mum tried to get me to eat some supper, but I didn't want any. I went straight to bed and fell asleep. François was keeping a lookout under a pine tree.

CHAPTER 10

On the last evening of the holidays, we got a call from the Marottes. They were coming back the next day. It was sad news but good timing, because François would only be on his own for one day.

Mum put the receiver down.

'Lucy, they want to hear that pooch.'

'A dog on the dog and bone!' I nearly joked. But then my temper got the better of me. 'He can't come now, he's busy. He's listening to *The Call of the Wild.*'

Mum shot me a dark look, but I wasn't giving in. Poor François! All right, so being made a fool of never killed anyone, but still, there are limits.

The next day, we were about to set out – my parents for work and me for school – when François plonked himself in front of the door, blocking our exit. Because he's tiny, it would have been easy to shift him, but the determination in his eyes filled me with respect. Rebellions and tears should be listened to: they're both cries from the heart.

I got it. François had every reason to be annoyed with me for deserting him. We'd spent a whole fortnight hand in paw, sharing everything, experiencing our joint wonder at the hugeness of the world together. And all it took was one ring of the school bell for me to desert him. I wasn't proud of myself. I looked down to show I was sorry, but what could I do? I stretched out my hand to stroke François, but Dad looked at his watch and kicked him out of the way. No time for social niceties now. I thought of pets abandoned by motorways and my heart skipped a beat. When it comes to animals it's always a race between the clock and hearts that wither before they can flower, because love takes time to blossom. I was starting to feel rebellious too, when something incredible happened: François lifted his leg, looked Dad straight in the eye and peed on the carpet. Wow, it was the first time he'd done something like that, and it wasn't an accident. He'd done it on purpose, a gigantic pee! I grabbed François before Dad could react. I had to rescue him from the biggest mess he'd got himself into to date. 'He doesn't want to stay behind on his own,' I said. 'I'm going to take him round to Theo's.' And, just like that, I left Dad to his temper and carried François off.

At 7 Rue Merlin, François swaggered through the open door. Grandpa was only too pleased to see him. I set off again with Theo, telling her about the victory we'd just scored. But there was no stopping François on his road to freedom.

When I went round that evening to collect him, Balthazar was in a total state. François had taken the open door as an invitation to travel: he'd disappeared, leaving Grandpa looking twenty years older.

'I've run from square to square, visited every butcher, checking out every patch of green,' he wailed, tearing his hair out, 'but nobody's seen him.'

Theo and I could feel our hearts sinking . . . Especially mine. The Marottes were due back this evening. What was I going to say to them? And as for my parents? The day had got off to a bad enough start as it was. I could already see Dad quoting Racine at me, 'O Lucy, beware my wrath!', his words poking me like a threatening branch, making me shudder all over. Then we both thought of Maougo, and immediately started running. Being a fairy, she'd know what to do.

Up on the fifth floor, Matthew was lining up his

Disney characters, Marie wasn't back yet and Maougo was stirring the contents of a saucepan.

We took it in turns (like we were singing a round) to give her a jumbled version of what had happened. She understood, even though it came out in a hotchpotch. I'm telling you, she's a fairy! It was almost as if she'd been waiting for us. And how about this for proof? With no advance warning, she turned the heat out under the saucepan. Now, I don't know what was simmering away, but there aren't many dishes you can just leave like that. They either burn, or stick to the bottom or turn out lumpy: one way or another, the food gets its revenge. But Maougo turned out the heat under the saucepan just as if she'd been expecting to, took off her apron and was all ours.

We went through into the landing. Matthew was there holding the tama: he'd already put his shoes on. Before we'd realised what was happening, he'd turned the key in the lock and sped off. Maougo reached after him – not to stop him, but to hold on to him. Matthew was going to lead the dance. We were hot on his heels.

* * *

It was six o'clock on a rainy January evening, and the streets were empty. Matthew crossed Rue de la Folie-Regnault and Rue de la Roquette to reach Père-Lachaise cemetery. He strode along with his head thrust forwards, as if he was being guided by his senses.

Ten past six, and the cemetery gate was closed. Matthew headed towards Rue du Repos which flanks the right-hand side of the cemetery. He wedged the drum under his arm like a megaphone. Rue du Repos was narrow and silent. The only noise was the sound of our footsteps. A road cleaner was sweeping up the rain. The night and the rain made a curtain over the earth. We looked like shadows. Suddenly, Matthew beat the tama. The cemetery wall was high, but the drum-beat rose up and straddled it. Matthew's hands were at top volume as he stomped the cobblestones. He was as strong as an engine. I brought up the rear. Love would win out. Love was stronger than the night.

The second entrance to the cemetery at 16 Rue du Repos was also closed. There was a raven on top, but it didn't move. It let out a cry, and I jumped. We carried on our way. At Rue de Bagnolet the cobbles gave way to tarmac. The road just kept on getting steeper, but Matthew didn't stop. He turned into Rue de la Reunion. There was a third entrance at the end. It was a stone porch with a triangular-shaped roof where some pigeons had clustered in a neat row, comfortable, warm. I'd often wondered where pigeons slept. Now at least I knew about six of them.

Without sparing a thought for the birds, Matthew stood right in front of them, beating his drum twice as hard. That won't do any good, I thought, banging on a drum won't open doors. But Matthew carried on, his body taut and his hands flying free. Up until then, he'd been drumming as he ran, scattering his notes like Tom Thumb – apart from in Rue de Bagnolet where his hands stayed quiet. So after a silent interval, interrupted only by the pouring rain, his drum-beat seemed even stronger. The cries of his hands made holes in the dark and silence.

Maougo didn't say anything. Nor did Theo and I. We were waiting, hanging on Matthew's gestures. I remembered the best bit from Jack London. *Obeying the call, he would spring to his feet and dash away, and on and on, for hours, under the fresh canopy of the forest …* What an idiot I'd been, how totally irresponsible. It was my fault François had gone off. Me and my ideas about freedom. Why had I wanted him to get back to nature? A tiny little dog like that. He wasn't Buck! He wasn't a St Bernard. He was a house dog with a flimsy coat of fur and meant to be mollycoddled. With the first cold snap, he needed to wear those little tartan coats that do up at the side.

The rain was still falling and I closed my eyes. We couldn't hear the cars any more. The drum-beat from the tama was flying. Behind the cemetery wall, the trees soaked up the water from the sky in a sweet-smelling symphony. I thought of Balthazar. You could have heard those sounds at the dawn of this planet, before life began. The whale song blended into what I was hearing because the sea mirrors the sky. Poor François, what had I done?

The world is a very big place. François didn't have a wild animal's instincts. He'd never find his way again. He hadn't got lost. *I'd* lost him.

I was drowning in guilt under the pelting rain when all of a sudden I thought I heard a noise, far off in the night, like a lost bark. Had I imagined it? Did I want it so badly I was hearing things? Had that bark risen up from the bottom of my guilty conscience?

I looked at Theo, she'd heard it too. And Maougo was frozen still. Now, one person might imagine things. But three people imagining the same thing at the same time?

Matthew started beating more energetically and my heart raced with the rhythm of his hands. It was still the same beat. Three times, the same cry in the night. Then he paused and we strained our ears, waiting for the echo . . .

Suddenly there it was, the barking sound. Far

away to start with, then getting closer. So close we nearly had to step back. It was François! He was there, just behind the wall. A little ball of a dog scampering along the wall, sending the leaves flying.

Theo and I threw ourselves at the wall, shouting at the tops of our voices. Maougo didn't move but something shifted in the way she was watching. She looked more relaxed. Matthew stepped back a few metres and started climbing the railings of the natural garden, with the tama on his back.

The natural garden is a park where flora and fauna live together in harmony. We went on a school trip there at the beginning of the year.

Matthew climbed like a monkey. He surprised me. I'd never met someone who could be so clumsy at times, and so agile at others. He straddled the bars and threw himself off, landing in the garden in a perfect drop shot before disappearing into the undergrowth.

Maougo pinned herself against the bars, making her body a stepping stone for us. I'm normally good at gym, but I landed in a big sprawl. Theo didn't manage any better, but she was laughing anyway so it didn't look as silly. The two of us were on the garden side now, and Maougo signalled to us to carry on. She'd wait for us in the street. I couldn't believe the railings were stopping her. There had to be a more mysterious reason separating her from us, probably something to do with magic. So I grabbed Theo's hand and we pushed our way through branches that skimmed our hair.

The combinatin of the night and the rain and the trees meant we couldn't see a thing. But our ears picked out Matthew. We crawled along, guided by the sound of the tama. I remembered what our science teacher had said on the trip: 'Bluebells flourish in the undergrowth, shaded by the trees. This is where the great tit chooses to make its nest. Growing in the walls and trellises and along the cemetery enclosure, you'll find an abundance of bindweed and clematis, their feathery fruit carried off by the wind. Daisies and tall grasses provide shade and cool for the snails and field mice in the grassland. There are newts in the pond. Mint, irises and marsh-loving forget-me-not grow on its banks . . .'

I imagined all those little creatures bustling about underneath me. We were on their patch, in a garden where human beings were only allowed during the daytime. By night, we were intruders and if you did an eye-count, there'd be thousands more of them than there were of us.

I held on to Theo's hand even more tightly. The sound of the tama was closer now. Suddenly, at a bend in the trees, there was Matthew and I could make out the drum on a bench. Matthew was facing the cemetery wall in one of the few places it wasn't covered in barbed wire. In that little clearing, surrounded by maple trees, elder trees and bramble bushes, he looked like an imp under the waterlogged full moon. His pale face stared in the direction of the stars while his hands carried on with their independent, frenetic life.

There was no let-up from the tama when, all of a sudden, the light darkened. Theo and I looked up. On top of the wall, the body of a dog stood out against the circle of the moon. François! He looked fantastic. Better than in the drawing with the caption. Motionless as a statue he looked at us and the shadow he cast on the ground was gigantic. It was more than just a silhouette. It represented a battle won.

We were very calm as we headed home. This time we were a full house. François was our common link, like a hyphen. He wasn't some crazy little dog who'd let freedom go to his head any more. He trotted along at a relaxed, responsible pace. It was as if running amok had helped him find his way again. He wasn't cut out for the wild life that Buck rejoined when he left behind the dog in him to become a wolf. His way was more that of a sheepdog rounding up stray members of the flock. As for Maougo, she was bringing up the rear again, singing words we couldn't understand in a deep voice, carrying us with the flow of them . . .

We entered Rue du Repos from the other end. It wasn't raining any more, it was streaming.

Back at 7 Rue Merlin, group hysteria had broken out. The entire family tree had taken root on the pavement: Fatoumata, Mamassa, Suleiman and Balthazar. When she saw her pet pooch looking so drenched, so handsome, and so different in front of number 11, Mrs Marotte nearly had a heart attack. As for my parents, I must have missed something, because there was another family row – surprise, surprise – and then somehow, search me how, they ended up arguing about the colour of the china dinner service they'd got as a wedding present before I was born!

Marie had been waiting on her own all that time up on the fifth floor, stirring the saucepan clockwise, in slow motion. That evening we said goodbye to François. Without suspecting anything, Mrs Marotte opened up her shopping bag. 'Jump in my little rabbit!' she said in a silly voice. But François didn't take any notice of her and walked off proudly. The landing light glowed softly and, like a lion in the savannah, he headed off peacefully into the sunset.

Last night, I got up to pin a star under my mezzanine bed. It stands for Matthew, who's a planet all to himself. In order to get to know that planet you have to do away with rules and prejudices and language, and throw yourself at it without being frightened of travelling through space. When I grow up, I want to teach autistic children. Matthew is my very own battle of the planets!

This morning, I popped up to Marie's before going to school. It was for Matthew's logbook. After yesterday's adventure, I wanted to know what kind of night he'd had. Maougo opened the door, and I said hello to her. When he heard my voice, Matthew came charging at me like a crazy dog, the Persian rug turned into a fast-flowing stream, and he shouted my name as he harpooned my hair.